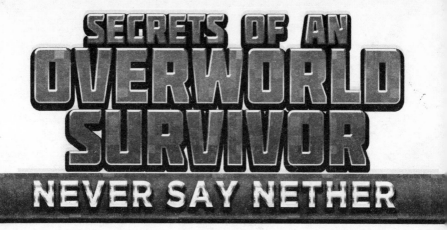

SECRETS OF AN OVERWORLD SURVIVOR

NEVER SAY NETHER

Also by Greyson Mann:

Secrets of an Overworld Survivor

Lost in the Jungle

When Lava Strikes

Wolves vs. Zombies

The Creeper Diaries

Mob School Survivor

Creeper's Got Talent

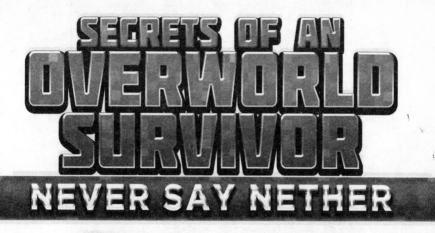

SECRETS OF AN OVERWORLD SURVIVOR

NEVER SAY NETHER

GREYSON MANN

ILLUSTRATED BY GRACE SANDFORD

Sky Pony Press
New York

SECRETS OF AN OVERWORLD SURVIVOR

NEVER SAY NETHER

CHAPTER 1

"You've been *where?*"

Will stared at Mina as if seeing her for the first time. She looked the same on the outside—a red-headed girl with determined green eyes. But he wondered what secrets and strengths she'd been hiding on the *inside*.

"I've been to the Nether," she repeated. "You can't brew potions without Nether wart. And that only grows in one place, Will."

She carefully placed another potion bottle on the low stone wall. They were sitting in an indoor garden, sun streaming through the windows in the roof above. The potions in Mina's glass bottles were as colorful as the poppies, roses, and sunflowers surrounding them.

"Ugh, I'm nearly out of potion of weakness *and* potion of healing," she said, shaking the contents of the last two bottles in her sack. "That zombie siege in Little Oak took almost everything I had."

Will glanced out the window at the charred fields of his brother Seth's farm. "The zombies took almost everything Seth had, too," he said. The indoor garden was one of the last green spaces near Little Oak."

"I guess I'll just have to go to the Nether and start over," said Mina with a sigh, sitting back on her heels.

Will shushed her with a finger. "Don't let Seth hear you say that. He'd freak out. He says people don't come back from the Nether." He searched the plants and bushes nearby, wondering where Seth was pruning now.

Mina shrugged. "Well, *I* came back, didn't I? And I will again—with plenty of Nether wart. And ghast tears, glowstone dust, blaze powder . . ." She

rattled off a list of potion ingredients as she slid her bottles back into her sack.

Ghast tears? Blaze powder? Will imagined the mobs Mina would have to fight to gather those ingredients. What an adventure! He sprang to his feet. "I'll go with you."

Mina shook her head. "Thanks, but like you said, Seth probably won't let you go."

Won't let *me go?* thought Will.
He'd already been to the jungle, the
Extreme Hills, and the Taiga. He
didn't need his brother's permission to
travel—he could go where he wanted.
He was about to tell Mina that when
the lilac bush across the cobblestone
path began to shimmy and shake.

"Creeper!" Will shouted, grabbing
his sword.

But instead of a green mob
exploding, a dark head popped up
from behind the bush. Seth wore
a muddy apron and held a pair of
pruning shears.

"It's okay with me if Will goes to
the Nether," he said calmly, as if he'd

been a part of the conversation all along. "And I want to go, too."

"Wait . . . what?" sputtered Will. "But you never go anywhere! You don't fight mobs. You stay here, and farm, and build things, and do stuff like . . . gardening." He pointed at the shears in Seth's gloved hands.

"I'm going with you," said Seth, more firmly this time. "You and Mina saved me from the zombies. Now it's my turn to repay you."

Will shook his head. "You don't have to do that. The Nether is full of ghasts and blazes. I mean, they're *way* more dangerous than zombies. Tell him, Mina!"

For some reason, Mina stayed silent. She studied her fingernails as if they were the most interesting things in the world.

"We'll fight the ghasts and blazes," said Seth, "if that's what we have to do. You and Mina can teach me how."

Seth's words bounced around in Will's mind: *You can teach me how.* He had never heard Seth say that before—about *anything.* He imagined what it would be like battling mobs beside Seth, teaching his brother how to fight off the quickest and strongest monsters. The thought made Will smile just a little.

Mina raised her eyes, waiting for his response. Seth stared at him, too.

Finally Will said, "Okay."

"Okay," said Mina with a grin. She held out her hand, palm down.

"Okay," said Seth, putting his hand over hers.

We're going to the Nether! thought Will. *This is my chance to show my brother what I can do.* He put his hand firmly on top of Seth's.

CHAPTER 2

"No," said Mina, pointing at the diamond pickaxe sticking out of Seth's pack. "You shouldn't bring your diamond tools, Seth. They're too valuable, and you'll end up losing them in lava or to an angry mob. Just bring iron ones—they're good enough for the Nether."

Will hid a smile. When it came to packing and planning, Seth was usually the one doing the scolding, not *being* scolded.

But then Mina pointed toward the water bowl in Will's hand. "You can't bring your dog, Will. Dogs can't go through the Nether portal. Besides, there's no water there. What would you pour in Buddy's bowl? Hot lava?"

From her dog bed in the corner, Buddy heard her name. She lifted her head and thumped her tail.

Will had tamed the wolf in the snowy Taiga, and Buddy was an amazing fighter. She could take down a zombie or even a skeleton in the blink of an eye—much quicker than Seth or even Mina could. And now Will had to leave her behind? It seemed so unfair!

"She can join the other wolves guarding Little Oak," said Seth. "In case the zombies come back."

Zombies, schmombies, thought Will. The zombie siege in Little Oak had been scary, for sure. *But wait till we get to the Nether. Then we'll battle some* really *hostile mobs,* he thought with a shiver of anticipation. He strapped his bow and arrow over his shoulder.

"I hope we have enough of these to last," said Mina, wrapping a few glass vials in cloth. "Potion of

fire resistance, especially. Lava is
everywhere in the Nether. I've heard
of explorers who stepped through the
Nether portal and fell right into it!"

"Really?" said Will. That
would be horrible luck—finally
reaching the Nether
and burning up in a
pit of lava after
just one step.
But the
only part
of Mina's
story that
Seth heard was
the word *portal*. "Can I help you build
it?" he asked.

Mina smiled. "I was hoping you'd offer," she said. "Nether portals aren't easy to build—they take lots of obsidian. But you're the best builder in Little Oak. You'll have it done in no time!"

Will felt the quick burn of jealousy. All his life, he'd heard people call Seth the "master builder." Will could hardly wait to get to the Nether, where building wasn't important—not as important as fighting, anyway.

"While you guys build that portal, I'll just . . . um . . . bring Buddy down to Little Oak," he said. The thought of saying goodbye to Buddy hurt his heart. But Will didn't want to stay here and help build the Nether portal. Seth didn't *need* his help—Will would just be in the way.

So he gathered Buddy's things, whistled for his dog to follow, and headed down the hill toward the village below.

When Will was only halfway back up the hill, he could already see the Nether portal. He shaded his eyes. It loomed toward the sky like a giant black picture frame with two figures standing inside.

Mina waved as he grew closer. "Isn't it amazing?" she called.

Will had to agree. Seth had laid out four blocks of black obsidian in a straight line. Two pillars of obsidian stretched upward from those, and another four blocks framed the top. But why were Seth and Mina already standing inside?

"Wait for me!" called Will, breaking into a jog.

Mina laughed. "It's not lit yet," she said. "We can hop through it all day long and never get to the Nether." She demonstrated by jumping through the portal and back again.

Still, Will raced up the hill, afraid of missing out on *something*. By the time he reached the portal, he was breathing hard.

"Do you want to do the honors?" asked Seth, handing him a flint stone and a C-shaped piece of steel.

Will shook his head. Building fires was like building houses—Seth was much better at it. "You do it," he said.

Seth struck the steel against the flint until it sparked to life. Then he

held it out toward the hollow space
of the Nether portal. Instantly, purple
flames leaped from the frame. Seth
jumped back and dropped the flint.
"Yikes!"

Mina sighed. "Isn't it beautiful?"

Will couldn't respond. He stood mesmerized by the swirling purple wall. Beads of sweat popped up on his forehead, but all he wanted to do was walk through that flame.

"Wait!" said Mina, pulling him back. "Not yet. You might be walking into a pit of lava, remember? Drink this first—a potion of fire resistance." She pulled a glass bottle filled with orange liquid from her sack. "This works for only three minutes. So after you drink it, you have to go through right away, okay?"

Will nodded and met his brother's eyes. "I'll go first, just in case," he said bravely. *Because this is what* I'm *good at,* he wanted to add.

"Wait!" said Seth. "I'm not ready. I dropped the flint." He squatted to pick it up from the ground.

Will laughed. "You won't need to build a fire where we're going, brother." But he wondered if Seth was *really* worried about the flint or just having second thoughts about the Nether.

Well, I'm not afraid, thought Will. *I'll protect him.* He took a deep breath—and the first tasteless gulp of potion. Then he handed the bottle back to Mina and eagerly stepped through the flames.

CHAPTER 3

Will opened his eyes to flickering lavender flames and quickly closed them again, his lids burning. As he inhaled heat and smoke, his lungs heaved. Without warning, he tumbled out of the portal, coughing and sputtering. The ground felt hot—too hot. *Lava?*

He jumped to his feet, relieved to see them firmly planted on some sort of reddish-orange rock. It was hot, all right, but it wasn't on fire.

The world around him was bathed in an orange glow. Flames shot up from the ground in random bursts, and lava streamed down from the ceiling into a swirling, bubbling pit. Will spun in a circle, taking it all in.

Then he realized he wasn't alone.

A man with a sword was quickly approaching. As he neared the lava pit, the fire cast light on his green flesh—*zombie* flesh.

Then the zombie turned his head, and Will saw splotches of pink, too. Now he knew exactly what he was dealing with—a zombie *pigman*. Will drew his sword.

When Seth tumbled out of the portal, Will didn't have time to think. He sprang into action, putting himself between the pigman and his brother. Will lunged at the monster, who squealed with surprise—then rage.

In an instant, he was sprinting toward Will. He was fast, *so* fast! This mob was *nothing* like zombies in the Overworld. Will realized in a heartbeat that he didn't know how to fight it. But if he kept running, he could at least lure it away from Seth.

Then he saw with horror that three more pigmen had joined the fight, sprinting from the flame-filled corners of the Nether. He and Seth were already outnumbered!

When another mob flew at Will from the side, he raised his sword.

"Will, it's me!"

Mina was running beside him, and when she turned to fight the grunting, snorting mob, Will found the courage to turn, too. Together, they knocked the pigmen backward. One fell into the lava pit with a hiss and a squeal.

Will lunged toward another pigman, striking him with his sword. Out of the corner of his eye, he saw Seth running toward them with his own sword drawn. That made Will strike harder and faster. Before Seth could even reach them, the zombie pigman was nothing more than a smoking heap of rotten flesh.

Seth's jaw hung open, his eyes wide and wild.

"I . . . I'm sorry I didn't get here in time to help," he said.

"It's okay," said Will, trying to catch his breath. He'd done it by himself—he'd protected Seth and shown him what a good fighter he could be. And Seth *did* look impressed.

But Mina sure didn't.

"Why did you *do* that?" she snapped at Will.

He took a step backward. "What? I saved Seth from the zombie pigmen. Why are you mad?" He raised his arms in confusion.

"You didn't *save* anyone from the pigmen," said Mina. "You put

us in danger. The pigmen wouldn't have bothered us if you hadn't attacked one. They're a passive mob. You don't have to fight everything you see, Will. The Nether is dangerous enough."

Sheesh, thought Will, sliding his sword back into its sheath. *Sorry.*

Five minutes into their Nether adventure, and he had already done something wrong. He hadn't tumbled out of the portal into a lava pit. *But I might as well have,* he thought sadly as he followed Mina back toward the portal.

"Seth, that's brilliant," said Mina, running her hands over a wall of Nether brick. "It's as solid as cobblestone, and it won't catch fire."

Seth beamed as he added another red stone to the wall.

Even in the Nether, he's a master builder, thought Will. His brother had spotted the best building material to create their base and was just finishing a wall around the portal.

"Score one for Seth," he mumbled.

Mina shot him an odd look. "What?"

"Nothing," he said. "Can I help?"

"As soon as Seth is done, you can help me explore the Nether fortress," said Mina. "We passed one while we were battling pigmen—did you see it? I could almost smell the Nether wart." She lifted her nose to the air, but the twinkle in her eye said she was joking.

Will *hadn't* seen the fortress. He'd been too busy trying to protect Seth. But he was itching to check it out now. "I'm just going to step outside and take a look."

Mina hesitated. "Don't go too far," she said. "Wait for us. There'll be ghasts protecting the fort."

She might as well have told him that the fort walls were made of diamonds.

Will had never seen a ghost before. His heart thudded with excitement.

So while Mina helped Seth finish his wall, Will stepped outside it into the depths of the Nether. He kept his eyes peeled for the enemy—he was good at that. And he spotted the fortress quickly, too.

Like a red-brick castle, its towers loomed above the cavern. Will imagined wither skeletons looking down on their fiery kingdom from the windows of those towers. Then he noticed they were connected by a bridge.

And floating right above that bridge, he saw his first ghast: huge, white, and fluffy. The jellyfish-like mob looked almost *friendly.* Its tentacle legs swayed back and forth as if waving hello to Will. Had it seen him?

Will let his guard down for only a second.

The ghast opened its mouth and launched its first fireball.

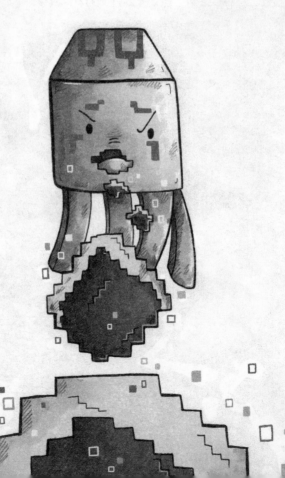

The ball of flame howled as it flew past Will and struck the ground behind him.

Missed me! he thought with relief.

Then he felt heat on his arm—and searing pain. As he glanced down he realized with horror that . . .

He was on *fire*.

CHAPTER 4

Water! was all Will could think. *I need water!*

Then he remembered he was in the one place where there *was* no water. He was in the Nether. And he was on his own.

He dropped to the ground and rolled over and over, narrowly missing a fire pit. When he sat up, his cape smoked and smoldered. The flames were out, but his arm throbbed with pain.

And the ghast was still firing from above.

Will dodged fireballs as he raced back to the safety of Seth's Nether brick walls. He dove to the ground, holding his arm and rocking back and forth.

"Get . . . the ghast," Will gasped.

Mina grabbed her bow and arrow and ducked behind the wall. She fired arrows, one after another, into the dark sky.

Will heard the screech of the ghast, which sounded *not* so friendly anymore. And when the screeching finally stopped and Mina darted out to collect the ghast tears, Will rolled onto his back with relief.

Seth dropped down beside Will.

"Did you hurt your arm?" he asked, carefully peeling back the smoking shards of Will's cape. When Seth caught sight of the burn, he turned his face away.

"Is it bad?" Will asked, afraid to look.

"It's bad," said Mina, hurrying back into the base. "But I can heal it, in time." She quickly pulled a purple potion from her sack. "Potion of regeneration. It doesn't work as quickly as potion of healing, but it'll have to do. And, believe it or not, it's made with ghast tears." She smiled as she held the vial to Will's lips.

He wrinkled his nose, afraid that ghast tears would taste gross and salty. But the potion smelled like watermelon, and he guzzled it right down, suddenly realizing how thirsty he had become. Mina's potions were the closest thing to water he'd find here in the Nether.

"Thanks," he said, wiping his mouth.

"Thank *you*," she said, holding up the ghast tears she had collected. "Now I can make more. But next time, Will, wait for us!"

Next time, he thought, holding his throbbing arm, *I think I will.*

Inside the Nether fortress, the air felt cooler. Will stopped to enjoy a faint breeze as he followed Seth and Mina down the long, dark hallway. His arm still stung, but the potion was beginning to work—at least, that was what Mina kept telling him.

Up ahead, Seth looked twitchy. He glanced nervously over his shoulder, as if a ghast or zombie pigman might pounce on him at any moment.

"Just look for a stairwell," Mina said gently, as if to distract him. "If we can find a stairwell, we'll find a Nether wart garden."

The word *garden* seemed to calm Seth down. He hurried past Mina around the corner ahead.

"Hey! Check it out!" he called.

"Did you find one?" asked Mina, racing after him.

"I think so, but . . . wait, something's wrong."

The tone of Seth's voice sent Will sprinting ahead, too. When he rounded the corner, there was his brother, stuck in what looked like a patch of grayish brown mud.

"I can't . . . move . . . my feet," said Seth, his eyes wide.

Will tore into the mud after his brother, determined to get him out. But as soon as his own feet hit the mud, they stopped. He tried to take a step— just a single step—but his feet seemed to suddenly weigh a thousand pounds.

"I'm stuck, too!" Will cried. So much for saving his brother. Was this quicksand? If it was, they were *both* going down . . .

CHAPTER 5

"Is it quicksand?" Will cried. "Mina, get us out!"

But Mina had turned away, her shoulders shaking. Was she crying? Will had never seen her cry before. If she had given up on him and Seth, there was no hope—none at all.

Panic seared through Will's chest like hot lava. He didn't know whether to scream for help or cry.

Then Mina turned around, and he saw that she was *laughing*. His fear instantly turned to frustration. "What's so funny?" he demanded to know. "Get us out of here!"

"I'm . . . sorry," Mina sputtered, trying to take a breath. "You just look so . . . funny. It's not quicksand, Will. It's *soul* sand. And you know what that means? Nether wart is nearby." She ran past the patch of soul sand and down another hallway. "There!" she cried. "I see a stairwell!"

"Wait, aren't you forgetting something?" Will called behind her.

Mina laughed again and raced back. "Sorry." She held out a hand toward Will and began to tug. Will discovered that he *could* walk through the soul sand, but it took an eternity to take just a few steps. When he finally reached dry ground, he turned around to help Seth out, too.

But Seth had somehow managed to make it out all on his own. He blew past Will and started jogging after Mina down the long red tunnel. "Where's the stairwell?" he called to her. "Do you see the Nether wart garden?"

At the end of the hall, Mina stopped suddenly and held out her arm. "Wait!" she whispered.

"What?" called Will. "What now?" He picked up his pace, afraid of missing something.

"Blazes!" said Mina. She sounded annoyed. "I see one just around the corner—over the stairwell. Get your weapons ready."

As Seth fumbled with his sword, Will squatted beside him and got his own bow and arrow ready. *Finally!* he thought. *Here's my chance to help Seth.*

Mina had already sent an arrow around the corner at the floating, flaming mob. She ducked back into the hall and whispered, "Wait for it. One, two, three . . ." Sure enough, the blaze sent three vicious fireballs in Mina's direction. As soon as they hit the wall above her, Mina rounded the corner and raced toward the stairs, keeping her head low.

"You ready?" asked Will.

Seth didn't respond. His sword quivered.

"I'll go first," said Will. "Just do what I do." He poked his head around the wall, aiming his crosshairs at the flaming mob hovering above the Nether brick staircase. He shot off an arrow—and after Mina's attack, one arrow was all it took. The blaze exploded and a golden blaze rod dropped to the steps below.

"You did it!" said Seth, sounding surprised.

But Mina's shouts at the base of the staircase meant the fight wasn't over yet.

"C'mon!" hollered Will, taking off down the stairs. At the bottom, he ran smack into Mina, who was coming back *up*.

"Blaze spawner!" she shouted. "Right by the garden. We'll *never* get close to the Nether wart now!"

Sure enough, as she spoke, another blaze popped out of the spawner.

Will heard the first fireball blast into the wall behind him.

The second bounced off the stairs.

And the third knocked him right off his feet.

CHAPTER 6

"Run!" shouted Mina. "I'll cover you!"

Will couldn't run. He tried to push himself up off the stairs, but the fireball had knocked the wind right out of him. As he finally sucked in a ragged breath, he realized: *Seth is missing.*

Will scrambled up and looked over the stone rail. Had Seth fallen to the garden below? No, but there was the blaze spawner—a small black cage with a flaming monster spinning inside. Another blaze popped out, launching into the sky just inches from his face. As he lurched backward, he saw Mina's arrow strike the fiery mob.

"Run!" she shouted again to Will. And now he could—and did.

As he raced back up the stairs to the safety of the Nether brick tunnel, he was relieved to find Seth there waiting for him.

"Are you okay?" Will asked, scanning his brother for injuries.

"Yeah," said Seth. "I was just thinking . . ."

"Thinking?" cried Will. "Who has time to think during a blaze attack?"

"I was thinking about how to contain that spawner," Seth continued. "I'm pretty sure I could build something."

Will laughed out loud. "You want to *build* something? Seth, we're in the Nether, not Little Oak."

But as Mina slid into the hall beside them, she was all ears. "You mean like a trap?" she asked.

Seth cocked his head. "Maybe."

"That would be *perfect*," said Mina, her eyes lighting up. "I could get to the Nether wart *and* collect blaze rods and glowstone dust from the trapped blazes!"

Yeah, perfect, thought Will, his spirits sinking. Even down here in the Nether, it was Seth who kept saving the day.

But I'm supposed to be the one saving him! thought Will miserably.

He set down his bow and arrow with a sigh. It didn't look like he was going to be needing them again any time soon.

"It's working!" cheered Mina.

Seth had created a "cage" around the spawner out of Nether brick. He'd left just a small window in the trap. As blazes popped out of the spawner, one by one, they had nowhere to go— except out the window. And Will had his bow and arrow aimed and ready.

"This is almost *too* easy," he said, faking a yawn. He fired another arrow at the window, and a glowing blaze rod bounced out and onto the ground below.

"Can I try?" asked Seth.

"Sure," said Will, taking a step back. "It's all yours." He handed Seth his bow and arrow.

"Can one of you help me gather Nether wart?" called Mina, who was already halfway to the garden. She carried her sack at her side.

Will expected Seth to jump at the chance, but he didn't. He seemed to be having too much fun shooting the blazes.

Really? thought Will. *Now you want to fight them?*

That meant Will was stuck with gardening. He trudged behind Mina toward the clusters of leafy red plants bursting out of the patch of soul sand.

"Watch out for wither skeletons," Mina called to Seth. "They sometimes spawn near blazes." Then she turned to Will. "And you—remember not to step in the soul sand!" She chuckled as she squatted by the first row of plants, but when Will didn't laugh, she glanced up at him. "What's wrong with you?"

"Nothing," Will said, tearing a Nether wart plant out of the dirt and stuffing

it into Mina's sack. "I'm just tired of Seth winning every battle."

"Huh?" Mina sat back on her heels.

Will wished he could take it back, but now it was too late. He took a deep breath and went on. "I just thought that down here, I could teach *him* something for a change. But I don't know how to build things like he does. I can't compete with him!"

Mina shook her head. "Who said it was a competition? Look at this place!" She waved her arm around. "In the Nether, it's not about winning or losing. It's about staying *alive*. And we have to work together to do that. So stop keeping score, okay?"

Will knew Mina was right. And now he felt ashamed. He could barely meet her eyes.

Suddenly, a dark figure stepped out of the shadows behind Mina.

A skeleton. That was what Will's mind told him it was, but it was so *black*. And it carried a heavy sword instead of a bow and arrow! Was this one of the wither skeletons Mina had warned Seth about?

Will tried to warn Mina, too, but his words seemed stuck in soul sand. He opened his mouth just as the skeleton raised its sword—and struck.

Mina's eyes widened in pain. Then she slumped to the ground like a withered Nether wart plant.

CHAPTER 7

"Seth!"

It came out like a croak. But Seth heard and came running.

"What happened?" he asked.

Will couldn't answer. He was battling the skeleton as if Mina's life depended on it. *And it might,* he realized.

He struck the wither skeleton again and again with his sword, but it kept coming. Will darted around the Nether wart garden, lunging toward the skeleton and then retreating.

When he saw that Seth had lifted Mina from the ground, Will screamed at him, "Run! Bring her back to the base!"

Seth ran toward the staircase. The last Will saw of Mina was her head slumped back in Seth's arms, her red ponytail skimming the steps below.

Whoosh! The wither skeleton's sword sliced the air, narrowly missing Will's nose. As he yelped and jumped backward, his sword clattered to the bricks below.

In one swoop, the skeleton gathered it up.

Will reached for his bow and arrow and then remembered it was gone—he had given it to Seth back at the blaze spawner!

Two realizations hit Will like fireballs: He was empty-handed, with no weapons at all. And *no one* was guarding the blaze spawner.

Sure enough, a fiery mob slipped through the window of the brick trap and streaked through the sky toward Will. He tripped backward over Mina's sack of Nether wart and nearly stumbled into the garden.

Just stay alive, he told himself, remembering Mina's words. *Stay out of the soul sand. And stay alive.*

But as he reached down to pick up the sack, an idea struck. He didn't know how to build brick traps like Seth's, but he had learned a thing or two about soul sand. So he ignored the blaze and lunged instead at the skeleton, taunting him.

As the skeleton sprinted forward, Will leaped over the Nether wart garden, praying he'd land on the other side of the soul sand. He did—just barely. But the skeleton stumbled right into it.

With a groan and a rattle, he tried to get out. But his bony limbs moved in slow motion.

"Take that, you bag of bones!" screamed Will, pumping his fist in the air.

But the blaze overhead was heating up. As the first few fireballs came raining down on Will, he turned and ran—tripping up the staircase, fleeing down the long halls of the fortress, and bursting out again into the flaming cavern of the Nether.

Where was the base? There! He raced toward the Nether brick wall— the solid wall that Seth had built to protect them. All he could think about was getting back to Mina and Seth.

We'll be okay if we're together, thought Will. He only hoped it was true.

Then he saw the ghast.

The white ghostlike mob hovered over the base, as if beckoning Will forward. Then it opened its mouth and unleashed a high-pitched scream.

The fireball headed directly for Will. His hand darted for his sword and then for his bow—for any weapon he could grab. But he had nothing!

So at the last moment, just before the fireball exploded in his face, Will drew back his arm. He swung his fist with fury and desperation.

Smack!

 He heard the explosion. Then the world went dark.

CHAPTER 8

"I don't know what to do!"

Will recognized the voice. It belonged
to Seth, and as darkness gave way to
light, his face came into view. His eyes
looked swollen. Had he been crying?

Will sat up with a start. "Where's
Mina?" Then he saw her, slumped
onto the Nether rack beside him. Her
face was pale as moonlight.

"I don't know how to help her!"
Seth cried.

"Potion!" Will shouted. "She needs one of her potions." He scrambled to her sack and pushed past handfuls of Nether wart leaves. He found two glass bottles wrapped in cloth at the bottom.

One of the bottles held purple liquid. The other held orange.

Will stared at Seth, trying to remember. "What are they? What did she use them for?"

Seth shook his head and shrugged. He seemed fresh out of ideas.

Will unscrewed the lid of the orange liquid and sniffed. Nothing. The bottle might as well have held water. He suddenly wished he'd paid attention all those times that Mina was talking about her "potion of this" or "splash potion of that." But he never had, because potions were *her* thing, like building was Seth's thing.

Will unscrewed the lid of the purple potion, which smelled familiar—like watermelon. And with that scent, it all

came back. "Potion
of regeneration!"
shouted Will.
"She needs this one.
Help me sit her up."

Mina moaned as
Seth propped her up
into a sitting position. Will raised the
vial to her lips and poured a few drops,
which rolled off her chin. But the smell
or the taste seemed to wake her up a
little. She opened her mouth and let
Will pour a few more drops inside.

As they lowered her back down
to the ground, Seth stared at Mina.
"How long does it take to work?" he
asked, his voice cracking.

Will shrugged. "It doesn't work right away," he said. "At least, it didn't on my burned arm."

He hadn't thought about that burn for hours now, but as he peeled back his clothing, he saw that it had begun to heal. Seth saw it, too, and his face relaxed. Now they knew that the potion *did* work. It was just a matter of time.

Mina's breathing sounded shallow. *Does she have enough time?* Will wondered.

He tried to remember everything she'd told him about healing. She was

always pushing Will to drink milk or
to eat more to keep his strength up.
"What do we have for food?" he asked.

"Mushrooms," Seth said, checking
his pack. "I can make mushroom stew."
He seemed relieved to have something
to do. He quickly filled three bowls
with red and brown mushrooms, which
he heated over a small pool of lava.

The smell made Will's mouth water.
He only wished he had a big glass of
ice water to drink with the stew.

Taking care of Mina took Will's
mind off his thirst, and it seemed to

help Seth, too. They took turns feeding her sips of stew, and slowly—*very slowly*—she began to come around.

"The Nether wart," were the first three words she said.

"It's fine," Will said. "It's here." He patted her sack.

Mina closed her eyes with relief. "Good," she said. "I dreamed that a ghast blew up the garden with a fireball."

Will hid his smile. "There might have been a ghast or two," he said. "And a wither skeleton."

"Will blew up a ghast with his bare hands," said Seth.

"What?" Mina's eyes opened wide.

Will turned, too. Was Seth making up stories now?

"Don't you remember?" Seth asked, gazing at Will with admiration.

Will slowly shook his head. "I remember the fireball," he said. "It was coming straight for me, and I grabbed my sword. I *tried* to grab my sword or my bow, but . . . I didn't have anything."

"Except your bare hands," Seth said, nodding. "I watched it over the wall—you hit that fireball with your hand and sent it right back up to the ghast. It exploded. Ghast tears fell like fireworks."

Mina pushed herself up to her elbows. "You really *did* that?" she said. "I've heard stories about fighting ghasts that way, but I'd never be brave enough to try it. Wow. Score one for Will." She smiled at him.

Will felt heat rise to his cheeks. "Who's keeping score?" he said with an embarrassed laugh. "I'm just glad to be alive. I'm glad we're *all* alive."

Mina nodded. "Let's keep it that way. We have the Nether wart. It's time to go home."

Home. The word warmed Will from the inside, like mushroom stew. But when he glanced back toward the portal, he instantly broke out in a cold sweat.

The black obsidian frame stood tall and strong, right where they'd left it. But inside?

The purple flames were *gone.*

CHAPTER 9

"What happened to the flame?" Mina cried, jumping to her feet.

The fear in her voice sent a chill down Will's spine. No flame meant the Nether portal wouldn't work. No Nether portal meant they couldn't go home. Were they *stuck* here in the Nether?

"It was the ghast fight," Seth said. "A fireball hit the portal. I watched the flames go out. I didn't know what to do!"

Mina shook her head. "There's nothing you could have done," she said. "When a ghost disables a portal, that's it—it's all over." She began to pace nervously, as if the friction of her feet on the Nether rack could light the spark again.

"We need flint and steel," Will said out loud. Then he remembered something. They *did* have flint and steel. At least, Seth did—wonderful, plan-ahead, pack-what-you-need Seth!

Seth realized it, too. He slid the flint and steel from his pocket and held them out as if they were precious emeralds.

Mina ran toward him and pulled him into a hug. Will joined her, wrapping his arms around his big brother and squeezing tight.

Score one for Seth, he thought happily.

"Careful!" Seth said, laughing and pulling away. "You're going to make me drop them."

"Don't light anything just yet," Mina said. "Let's make sure we pack up everything we need."

As Will watched Mina pack up her Nether wart, blaze rods, ghast tears, and glowstone, he could barely stand the wait. Packing to go home was a *lot* easier than packing to go to the Nether. He had lost his weapons—his bow and arrow and his sword. But he wasn't even tempted to go back to the fortress to look for them.

I have everything I need right here, he thought, staring at Mina and Seth.

Finally it was time to light the portal. This time, Will let Seth show him how to use the flint and steel. He struck the C-shaped piece of steel against the flint stone again and again, but nothing happened.

"Think of the way you struck that ghast with your bare hand," Seth reminded him.

That did the trick. With one more strike, the flint started to smoke in Will's hand.

He held it toward the Nether portal
opening, which exploded into a
swirling purple mass.

"Wait!" Seth said.

"What now?" Will asked.

"Don't we need to drink that orange
stuff first?"

"Potion of fire resistance?" Mina asked. "No, I don't think we're going to land in a pit of lava when we step back into the Overworld." She grinned.

"*That's* what the other potion was!" Will said. "We couldn't remember— when you were sick. We were pretty worthless without you, Mina."

"You kept me alive," she said solemnly. "So I must have taught you guys something." She winked and then stepped through the purple flame.

Seth hurried up onto the obsidian, as if he were afraid of being left behind.

"Do you want to go next?" Will asked.

Seth nodded, grinned, and disappeared in a poof of purple.

So that left Will alone in the Nether. He took one last look at the lava-streaked walls and the seemingly bottomless pit of fire. When he heard a *snort* coming from the other side of the brick wall, he froze, wondering if he'd imagined it.

Then the zombie pigman stepped into view.

Will reached for his sword. Drawing a weapon was as natural to him as breathing.

But then he remembered: He didn't *have* a weapon.

Mina had told him that the pigmen were passive mobs. Was she right about that? If Will left this monster alone, would he leave Will alone, too?

He held his breath as the zombie pigman walked toward the portal, snorting and squealing.

Then Will couldn't hold out any longer. He turned away and dove through the purple flames after his friends.

The air on the other side of the portal felt cool and dark. Night was falling on the hill above Little Oak. Will tumbled into the grass and inhaled deeply. The wet earth smelled like *home.*

He pushed himself to his feet, searching the hillside for Seth and Mina. There they were!

Mina was gesturing wildly at something behind Will.

Seth just stared.

At what? wondered Will. He whirled around to face the portal.

Something was walking across the wet grass. A man? A zombie?

No.

It was the zombie *pigman*.

CHAPTER 10

"Did he come through the portal?" cried Will, rushing to join Seth and Mina.

"Maybe," said Mina. "Or he spawned beside it. I heard that could happen."

Will was surprised to see Seth reach for his sword. "Don't hurt it!" Will shouted, holding up his hands like stop signs.

"But . . . we can't just leave it out here," said Seth. "Can you throw a potion at it, Mina?"

She shrugged. "I don't have any more potions of weakness. Can you build a trap or something?"

Seth scratched his head. "But what would I do with him once I trapped him?"

Will watched the pigman wander off toward the hills. "No potions or traps," he said. "I think we should just let this guy live—or at least explore the Overworld the way we explored the Nether. He'll probably run into a hostile mob before morning anyway."

Mina widened her eyes. "Listen to *you* now," she said. "All right, we'll let it live. But let's disable the portal."

While Seth chipped away at the obsidian frame, Mina took another

look at the potion ingredients she had gathered in the Nether.

"Did you get a lot of Nether wart?" asked Will.

Mina blew out a breath. "Not a lot. I guess our harvest was interrupted, right?"

Will shivered, remembering the battle with the wither skeleton. "Does that mean you have to go back to the Nether?" He almost hated to ask.

Mina shook her head. "Not anytime soon, anyway."

Will sighed. "The way I feel right now, *never* might be too soon."

"Never say never," Seth said, slinging his pickaxe over his shoulder as he joined them. "Or should I say, never say *Nether*?"

Will laughed out loud. But by the look on Seth's face, he could tell that his brother had already moved past the joke and was working on a new idea.

"Hey, maybe we can plant some of that Nether wart in my garden," Seth said to Mina. "I could build a wall around it to keep it safe."

Mina looked doubtful. "We could *try*," she said.

Will chimed right in. "You should let Seth help you," he said. "His ideas usually work—you know that. And he's a really good gardener."

"I'll plant the Nether wart and build the garden wall if you brew the potions," Seth said. "Deal?" He held out his hand toward Mina.

Instead of shaking it, Mina held out her hand palm down. "I'll brew the potions if Will fights my mobs for me. Deal?" She grinned at Will.

Will put his hand on hers. And this time, he let Seth put his hand on top.

We all have different talents, Will thought with a smile. *But together, we make a great team.*

"Deal," he and Seth said, at exactly the same time.